I0727937

STICKS AND STONES...

and Words

THAT HURT ME

A Collection of Poetry and Short Stories in
Support of
Domestic Violence Awareness

Edited by
Aurelia Maria Casey

STICKS AND STONES…

and Words

THAT HURT ME

Copyright Notice

TABLE OF CONTENTS

PUBLISHER'S NOTE

Any resemblance to factual events, people, or places is coincidental in the fictional poetry and short stories included in this anthology. Any personally identifiable information in the memoir and creative non-fiction poetry and short stories has been eliminated or changed in order to protect the innocent from the guilty.

The publisher is not responsible for reader's emotional reactions to the material presented in this anthology.

For all victims and survivors of domestic violence, wherever you are.

"It's the children the world almost breaks who grow up to save it."
— Frank Warren

EDITOR'S NOTE

Every October, people in the US come together for National Domestic Violence Awareness Month, and on college campuses across the country you can see posters with statistics about domestic violence. Personally, I don't find numbers alone to be particularly helpful, especially after taking my college statistics course and learning how difficult it is to interpret what any given statistic really means without going into an in-depth study of where that number came from. It's too easy to think that everyone you know is the exception, even though the statistics say otherwise.

However, statistics can be very powerful, especially when they help to tell a meaningful story. So that is what I have tried to do with this anthology. I have interspersed statistics with the poetry and short stories to enhance the meaning of both the numbers and the stories.

If you are a victim of domestic violence, I hope that reading this gives you courage. You aren't alone and there are people who wish you well, whole and safe. There is a section of resources at the end, with my opinion of the pros and cons of each, if you are ready to take action. If you aren't ready, listen to some uplifting music and know that there are people waiting to help you once you are ready.

If you aren't a victim of domestic violence, I hope that reading this gives you a better understanding of the harm that domestic violence in all it's forms can cause. Even after a victim has left his or her abusive environment, negative cycles can continue. Experiencing or witnessing domestic violence can lead to many health issues, both physical and psychological. This includes children with reactive attachment disorder (RAD), who are very likely to become abusers if they don't get the help they need. Most cases of RAD are misdiagnosed as ADD, ADHD, or other behavioral problems when in reality it is a trust issue often resulting from domestic violence and abuse.

Domestic violence is often hidden; a taboo subject. It is the silent secret that destroys lives, livelihoods, and families. Help break this cycle. Encourage people to talk about these issues and get help if they need it.

Best Wishes,

Aurelia Maria Casey

Most domestic violence incidents are never reported.*

"I want to believe that I'm not wrong. I want to believe that life isn't full of darkness. Even if storms come to pass, the sun will shine again. No matter how painful and hard the rain may beat down on me."

— Natsuki Takaya

EMBRYONIC COGNITION

By *Paul White*

I am so warm and comfortable here,
Snuggled up with you, my mummy dear.
I can feel your heart, each single beat
And sense your breath, oh so sweet
And when you speak, your voice I hear
So soothing in my little ear.

Then you start, jump upright
Your blood pumping with the fright
He is here again, I hear him shout
Now you're trembling, shaking about
Your tummy clenches, I'm held so tight
So I start to kick with all my might.

There's nothing more that I can do
But touch my hands and pray for you.

That last time, my brother died
He was in behind me, on the inside.
Hidden from sight, hidden from view
In the shadows, the nurses never knew.

So don't let daddy kill me, tell him leave me
    alone
I don't want to die yet, I've not even grown
Now I feel you turn, I feel you twist
As his hands you fight, you try to resist
While back and forth I am thrown
Then suddenly all goes quiet, are we alone?

His has done his bit, it's time to go,
But not before that last, vicious blow.
Now you cry, you're mortified
And you pray that all's well, on the inside.
So I kick and wriggle to let you know,
That I'm still here, your loving little embryo.

BIRTH IS A BETRAYAL

By Amelia Golden

Birth is a betrayal.

I did not ask
to be cut off
from our oneness,
from our ever-present,
ever-eternal
dynamic symphony,
one with we-warmth.

I did not ask
for cold, dark,
bitter blackness.

I did not ask
for loneliness,

for the existential realization
that only I
can know my own
thoughts and feelings,
that only I
can sense and digest
my particulated experiences.

I did not ask
to take on this heavy flesh,
immobile bones
and sluggish organs.
How many months
I struggled
to control my limbs.
How many years
to master speech.
How many lives
to master relationship?

I did not ask
for the succession of
meaningless tasks
that makes up so much of life.

I did not ask
for this smallness,
this insignificance,
cut off from embedded meaning.

I did not ask
for hatred,
betrayal,
neglect,
war.

I did not ask
for the scorn of others,
the mocking cruelty,
the permeating apathy.

I did not ask
for guilt,
for responsibilities
beyond my measure.

I did not ask
to carry the cross

of every deed and thought and feeling
I have ever individuated.

I did not ask
to be expected to
carry the cross for others
so that we can all
make movement
through eternity.

I did not ask
for this time,
for these people,
for this work.

I did not ask
to be ripped from
that which sustains me,
from the light and love
that lives in cosmic warmth.

I did not ask
to be silenced,
to hear the angels no more,

to delight in no spirits,
but merely to be confronted
with opaque matter,
ugly sharp-edged forms,
the need to eat.

I did not ask
for birth.

Yet I did long
for love,
I did thirst
for freedom,
I did desire
that all should thrive.
And if birth
is necessary
for these,
then,
at least
I can look forward
to death.

PAIN

By L. Meadow

I cowered between
the stove and wall
Again the pain
You, giant man, shouting
Mother standing between us
Again, the pain
Fist against flesh
Hands against ears
STOP!
Never again, this pain

RIVERS AND MOUNTAINS

By A.C.

August (The mid-Sixties)

It's been a few months. I'm still at my aunt
and uncle's place. It is in the country. I like the
big river nearby. They argue but don't fight like
mum and dad. They have two cats and a dog.
It's nice.

October

Back with mum and dad. They fought again.
It started because dad was eating the food aunt
and uncle had packed for us. He laughed when
mum asked him to give me some. It was worse
than usual. He punched mum in the eye. I tried
to stop it. Dad picked me up and took me next

door.

November (4 days later)

Back at aunt and uncle's.
Hooray! Off to the funfair again tonight!

(Later)

Didn't go to the funfair.
I'm on a train with mum. Reading my comic book. No-one said what's going on as usual. We just left. I want to go home.

Next Day

Still don't know where I am. Didn't sleep. Banged my head on the pillow until the guard opened the curtains. Tired but quite excited —there were mountains with snow outside the window!! I'm watching the people at the stations selling things to passengers.

Mum's black eye is very bad. She is wearing sunglasses and people keep looking at her.

(Later)

Here at last. It's London. I've been here before. My brother is here, as well as some other people. I'm not sure who they are. Mum seems quite happy to see them. It's really cold, everything is black or grey and everyone looks miserable. Not saying much. I still want to go home.

Two weeks later

Still confused but I know we have to be here. Hope I can go home soon. I miss the cats.

I don't like this place. At home we had fruit trees and flowers. We had fresh peaches every day. Here, I don't understand what people are saying and they think I'm stupid! My brother is alright. We get on. I haven't told him about anything because he's younger than me.

The adults (mum, her mum and her brother) whisper a lot when we're around. Why do adults always do this? I was there and I can tell what they're saying. No-one is interested in what I know. I don't care—I wouldn't tell them anyway. It only causes trouble.

Starting school tomorrow.

Next Day

School was OK. The kids were quite friendly but they didn't understand. I worked out they were asking why my skin is dark. I tried to explain it was because of the sunshine and it will go away again but it was too hard. They don't get much sunshine here. It just rains.

A Week Later

We met some people who lived somewhere else in London. There was a big river! No-one had said it was there. I watched it until we had to go. It helps, knowing there's a river. When will I go home?

ONLY YES MEANS YES

By *Aurelia Maria Casey*

We met at a party
You got me drunk
We danced and danced.
You took me home
You had sex with me
You thought I consented
I just didn't know how to say no.

We went to coffee
I called you a hunk
We laughed and laughed.
You took me home
I thought you loved me
You thought me demented
How could I know?

I finally got free
Of you, you skunk
I cried and cried.
Nowhere to call home
Nobody believed me
They all thought I consented
While inside I was screaming NO!

Around the world, at least one in every three women has been beaten, coerced into sex or otherwise abused during her lifetime. Most often, the abuser is a member of her own family.**

"Look. I have a strategy. Why expect anything? If you don't expect anything, you don't get disappointed."
— Patricia McCormick

SAFETY

By L. Meadow

Here in the dark
In the cupboard
Amongst my shoes
Clothes hanging dark
Above my head
I am safe
Cannot find me
Cannot hear me
Cannot hit me
NO! NO! NO!
It was safe
In the cupboard womb
Nowhere is safe
With you around
Leave me! Please!
Here in the dark

NIGHT SONG

By A. C.

The kids aren't alright.
The kids aren't alright.
Their parents are fighting again in the night.
One kid's in the corner
The other's upstairs.
Their daddy is dragging their mum by her hair.

The kids aren't alright.
The kids aren't alright.
They're hearing the sirens.They're seeing blue
    lights.
Their daddy is crying.
Their mother is dead.
Joe's teddy is covered in blood by her head.

The kids weren't alright.

The kids weren't alright.
Joe's going to prison -
He got in a fight.
"He's just like his father" the neighbours declare
While Sis hides her bruises and scratches from
    sight.

The kids aren't alright.
The kids aren't alright!
All over the world - the kids aren't alright.
They need intervention and people who care
Not neighbours who gossip and whisper and
    stare.

SHE STANDS AGAINST THE WALL

By *Amelia Golden*

She stands against the wall, cowering in the corner. Backlit in grey tones by weak light coming through the window. Her arms are frozen slack in towards her body. On the right her arm and shoulder huddle against an over-flowing bookcase. His books. Dusty volumes. Stacks on top, disorganized. She is as close to the bookcase as she can get, perhaps to avoid the bed—the marital bed, the big double bed. His bed. Her bed. With three icons of saints on the wall above as if to sanctify what happens in this place. The four walls hem in. The room is not much larger than the bed; one can just skooch around with the furniture against the walls. The TV is in this room. So sometimes, it is a public room, with bodies piled on the bed looking at the box on top of the dresser, with antennae. But now, it is clearly a private room. Where is everybody? It is not late enough for everyone to be in bed yet, so where are they? Where is the noise and bustle of the other eight bodies who live in this house/prison? Of course, this is private space; children are not allowed to enter here unless invited. I guess she must have been invited, or dragged, or threatened, or nudged. She is terrified. Her eyes are wide and do not blink. The shaking of her limbs is severely inhibited, in fear of incurring extra wrath. Her hair is thin, straggles around her face, but is nonetheless beautiful as it is lit up by the light from the window, like a miniature halo. She is not sure how long she can stay present. He stands there, five or six feet away. The door is closed, locked. Trapped. It is meaningless to search the room for escape, this she has learned long ago. She wants to sink into the wall, become invisible, cease existing. She feels the ledge of the window on her back. She knows if she leaned back, her head would feel the soft curtains and then the hard, cold glass.

She doesn't really look at him. She vowed long ago never to see his face, and she doesn't. She knows the military crew cut sticking straight up with thick spined hairs is there. The weak chin and disgusting, slim-lipped mouth. But she does not see it. The door is shut, and he has slunk off his pants, belt and change clanging. Skinny legs, pinstripe boxers. She will not see his hands. She will not see him approach. It is time, quickly. Quickly. Before another inhale. Out! Out! Outside somewhere is the dogwood tree that is her haven in times of absence. It is so cold out there! But in here is terror. She hears his sock-footed approach, some mumbled coaxing words. It is an old script, repeated indefinitely though it never produces the desired results. Her eyes are cast down as she shrinks as small as she can be. His arms come out. Her arms startle and jump of their own accord. She cannot control them. It is not her there. It is some thing, some body, some possession of that possessed man. She is already fading out. He has lifted her onto the bed. A deeply anticipating gaze strips her bare, though she does not see. She is gone; she has never been; nor will ever be.

She comes to, at some time, what time? It has darkened. She is lying on the bed—her father's side. She sees the ceiling with its little cracks and bumps. The simple square glass overhead light, off. He is gone. There are no sounds in this room, though murmurs of activity can be heard in the house. Is it dinnertime? Often, no-one notices if she is a bit late. She rarely gets enough to eat in any case, no matter when she shows up. She is still frozen, but starting to come to. Her eyes turn up and she stares upside down at the icons of three saints. What are they doing here, looking over this scene? Surely they do not condone the violations that occur in this room. The empty feelingless fucking of disembodied girl-flesh. So small, so innocent, so submissive. And quiet. That has long since been assured. But what are those saints doing here? Aren't they supposed to be good, bring comfort, protect? Here, all is wooden and simulacra only. Reality is relative, says Einstein from his picture across the room. She doesn't know if she has the strength to get up. She doesn't have the stomach for dinner. She isn't in fact truly here. Perhaps a marionetteer will appear and make her legs and arms perform the needed actions to reassemble her dress, cover those things under her torso, perhaps even find the balance to stand on them. There is ringing in her ears, and she almost faints again. But she must, she must let the marionetteer work her neck, arms, and legs. Sullenly and shrunken she pads out the door, quieter than a mouse. Go around the front, so no one knows that she has not just come from that room. Keep the gaze down. Sit on the chair like one is told to. Legs limply hanging. A plate is put in front of her. Her bile rises in disgust. She can take nothing more into her body. She pushes the food around on her plate. She is forced to eat. But it will not be digested. No one sees her tears, for they are not allowed to seep out from her conjunctiva. All is dry and empty. Bones and a little flesh. A little white flesh, once pure, once pristine. Now lacking in meaning. Lacking in blood. Lacking in ownership. She is forced to drink milk. Her body is allergic to it, and her intestines react quite soon with inflammation, gas, diarrhea. The stains in her underwear, if they are ever noticed, will not be thought about. Though if anyone looked, the signs of dried blood could be clearly differentiated from stool leakage and urine. Just another unwanted item on the colossal heaps of laundry to be dealt with in the basement. She knows the rank odor well, for she herself has hidden in that pile in desperate attempts not to be found. It is hard in a house of ten to be alone, to hide, to be left alone, to be sacrosanct.

Her bed is upstairs now. Finally, she has been removed/rearranged out of the little front room downstairs, the room where all this began and eternity thrust its spear through her beatless heart. Perhaps he won't come up tonight in padded feet, the stairs squeaking. Breath held to hear which way he might turn. But no, not tonight. He has had his fill, and he must fill the side of that bed with the saints overhead, pretending perfect Catholic union with his passive, exhausted, numbed perfect pseudo-Catholic wife.

It is nonetheless a long time before she can sleep. She curls up tight and freezes in her bed. Her face always towards the wall. She hears the sound of her sister sleeping in the big bed across the room. Other sounds to fear. But softly, carefully, she can hear the rustle of the leaves of the maple tree out back. The protective tree outside her bedroom window. It is tall and strong and does not let the passing deeds of humans disturb its growth and cycling of seasons. The leaves are still green, edging yellow in anticipation of fall. The air cools. Many stories, of fairies and leprechauns, of children, of stuffed animals come alive, of heroic actions, of suspenseful moments, of dire fear flit through her skull, some tracing story-threads, other just images desperately clung to only to dissemble in the night's fall. She will sleep. Her body will try to grow. She will survive, somehow, as she has until now. But she will not know who she is. For she is just a tool of others' fantasies.

WHY

By *Mimi Blake*

Because I always looked good in black and
   blue
Because you told me you knew I loved you
   before I told myself
Because love is patient
Because being shoved into a wall isn't really
   an abusive relationship
And neither is being dragged by a car
Because white picket fences take time to build
Because I could always warm my hands on
   my face when the heat got shut off
Because if it wasn't you it would be someone
   else
Because I liked your laugh on good days
Because your mom would send me flowers
   and no-one ever did that for me before

Because we had inside jokes

Because I thought I could love you through it

Because you taught my little girl to swim in
    the ocean

Because my mom had done worse and I still
    had her in my life

Because on some days the thought of dying
    was welcomed and you never liked to
    break a promise

Because I convinced myself that sorry was
    enough

Because I let you convince me that I wasn't
    enough

But now I know differently

MAGIC WORDS

By L. Meadow

Abracadabra
Hocus Pocus
Alakazam
Have no magic
But these words do:

"I'm leaving"
"Never coming back"
"Goodbye"
"Divorce is final"

Abracadabra
Hocus Pocus
Alakazam
Have no magic
But these words do:

"I am strong"
"I am whole"
"I am free"
"I am me"

QUINCEAÑERA

By *Aurelia Maria Casey*

Gabriela Maria Jones Martinez sat in her little nook in the corner of the roof. They were arguing again, Mama and Papa. She hated calling him that, since he wasn't actually her father, but he insisted. He beat her often enough when she remembered to call him Papa that she tried not to forget. She spent most of her nights up here on the roof of their little apartment in the slums of Cartagena. From here she could see the lights from the clean parts of the city—the places the tourists would go—as the sun set. It was a different world there. Sometimes she tried to wander through that part of the city. Everyone who looked at her knew she didn't belong, and inevitably one of the *tombos* would shoo her back here.

Here wasn't really home, so she never called it that. The other children, her half–siblings and the neighborhood kids, they called her *ojos azules*. Her eyes were blue, so she wouldn't have minded except they were cruel to her. Her real father was a police officer somewhere in the United States and the other kids were jealous because she was a US citizen. It didn't matter to them that her father had left her and Mama here when she was born. He had been in the military back then, and when she found him online a couple years ago he told her he hadn't known he would leave and then he was injured and by then it was too late: Mama had already married Papa. Whenever she had a few coins that Papa hadn't already taken from her she would go to the internet cafe and email her father. At least he seemed to genuinely care for her, if only from a distance. Papa despised her because she was an extra mouth to feed.

Mama had married Papa before she could remember: only a year or two after she was born. She wanted to leave, to go live with her father in the US, but she didn't want to leave

Mama. Her siblings all sided with Papa so she was the only one who protected Mama. Besides, her father didn't want her there, not really. He'd never even invited her to visit.

As the sky darkened, the dirty ugliness of the poor neighborhoods faded into shadow. All that was left was the electric glow of the high rises in the affluent sectors—the places tourists went to "experience Colombia." The apartments there were colorfully painted and carefully kept bright and vibrant. They had lived there once, when she was little. She barely remembered it now; it seemed like someone else's life. Papa had had a good job then, and was nice to her and Mama. He didn't become angry and violent until later, after he had lost a few jobs and could hardly afford food. He insisted that Mama couldn't work, so they had moved into worse and worse places and he had become crueler with every move.

It was warm, as usual, so she curled up on the roof where she had been sitting. She rested her head on her arm and tried to ignore Papa's yelling. She was still awake when the sounds of the night quieted. Her siblings had been put to sleep and Mama and Papa had gone to bed too. The occasional noises of people in the distance made a soothing counterpoint to the howling of cats, skittering of lizards, and humming of bugs. Eventually she slept.

Brett Jones sat in a rolling swivel–chair at the metal desk and tried to concentrate on the paperwork he was supposed to be filling out. People always thought that police work was all about catching the bad guys or terrorizing the citizenry over every little thing, but the reality was that about half of his job he spent writing reports. He was especially distracted today because Gabriella was turning fifteen soon and he wasn't sure that she would be safe living with her mother in Cartagena. He'd seen what went on in the shadowed alleyways back when he'd been in the army there.

It was late, most of the other officers on his shift had left already. The night shift was busy out front or on patrol. His only company was Maria, the precinct's janitor, who was working her way around the desks.

"Tell me, Maria," he said, "what are birthdays like in Colombia? Birthdays for kids, I mean."

"Your daughter?"

"Yeah."

"How many years?"

"Wha'dya mean?"

"She has how many years?"

"She'll be fifteen in a few weeks."

"Ah!" She smiled. "Quinceañera. Is a special day."

"What's kinsaynera?"

"Fifteen. Very special year. Big party. She woman now, not girl."

"Like a sweet sixteen?"

"Sí y no." She smiled, not sure how to describe the coming–of–age party that all Colombian girls had when they turned fifteen. "You go to Colombia for her?"

"No. She didn't ask me to. She didn't even tell me it was a big deal."

"Ah. Es very big deal. You see this?" she pulled out the gold chain she always wore. "Mi Papa he gave me this for mi Quinceaera."

"You get jewelry?"

"Sí. Y zapatos."

"Shoes? Like fancy shoes?"

"Sí."

"I wonder why she didn't tell me about it."

It was Sunday. They all sat, squished, around the small table while Papa said the prayer. They had rice and beans, but nothing else. They each had a small bowlful, the extra in the pot in the center. They ate in silence, waiting until Papa had eaten enough before Mama shared the rest among the six of them.

"Papa." Mama hesitated, looking at Gabriela.

"Papa will we have Quinceañera for Gabi?" asked her younger sister Ana.

"No."

"But—" Mama started, a worried frown wrinkling her forehead.

"I said no." He slammed his hands down on the table and stood up.

"Quinceañera is special, Papa." Ana said.

"What, you can't speak for yourself, girl? You make your Mama and Ana ask for you? You're the one always causing problems."

"Papa. Don't—" Mama's sentence was cut off when Papa slapped her.

"I should never have let you keep the gringo's bastard." Papa grabbed the back of her neck and lifted her almost off the floor. Mama was crying. Silent. Hoping he wouldn't do anything worse than a few punches. She sent Ana and the others into the bedroom they all shared.

"Out! I don't ever want to see your face here again. You understand? Never come back." He dragged her to the doorway.

"Mama! Mama I don't want to go without you!" That earned her an extra punch and a kick in the gut that sent her tumbling down the steps. The street—really more of an alleyway, twisting and curving down the steep hillside— was cobbled with steps to make it easier to climb up.

Once she was out of Papa's sight, she paused to catch her breath. Her stomach churned, her whole belly aching from that last kick, and she vomited. There wasn't much to come up, since she hadn't eaten much of the rice and beans in the first place.

"Gabi!" She looked up: it was Ana, running towards her with something in her hands.

"Ana. Why did you follow? You know Papa will only hurt you for it."

"Mama said to give you this. She was saving it to get your dress and shoes for your party."

Gabriela took the folded handkerchief full of pesos and hugged Ana.

"Go through the roof. That way you can say you were sitting up there the whole time."

Ana ran back up the street. Gabriela sighed. Mama had saved enough to take her to the US Embassy in Bogotá. She started walking towards the bus station, looking back every now and then. She hoped Papa or Mama would come tell her to come home again, but she didn't expect to see them. Mama wouldn't leave, not now that Papa had five children tying her to him, stronger even than their wedding vows. She hoped Ana would take care of Mama, but she was only ten, sheltered and spoiled. Papa's favorite.

The rickety old bus was full of men. They

smelled like sweat and beer and they were probably all going to the capital looking for temporary work. She ignored them and sat next to an old woman, likely a grandmother traveling to visit her children and grandchildren. Or coming from visiting them.

The bus would take at least 16 hours to get to Bogotá. She settled in and tried to sleep. She woke up at every strange noise and jolt, and by the time they arrived in she was tired and stiff in addition to dirty and bruised. When she got out of the bus, she asked the man behind the counter at the bus station how to get to the US Embassy.

Gabriela stood and looked at the US Embassy. The guards wore camouflage and held machine guns. There was already a line, waiting. She was afraid to go in, but it was her best option, so she walked past the guards and joined the line, which moved very slowly.

It was cool and clean inside. It took her eyes a minute to adjust to the harsh fluorescent lighting. Finally it was her turn.

"How may I help you?" asked the woman.

She licked her lips and tucked a loose strand of hair back behind her ear.

"I need papers," she said in English. "To visit my Dad."

"You need a non–immigration visa?"

"I'm not sure."

"We don't give Colombian identification here. This is a US Embassy. If you want to visit the US you need a non–immigration visa. If you're moving there then you need an immigration visa."

"Do I need a visa if I'm a citizen? My dad— he's American. He's a police officer in Dallas."

"Do you have proof of US citizenship?"

"No."

"A birth certificate or a passport?"

"No. I came here for that."

"I can't help you without some proof of identification. I'm going to have to ask you to leave."

Dazed, she left, ignoring the military guards completely. She wandered aimlessly for a while. She didn't really know where anything was in Bogotá; after all, she'd never been there before.

Most of the buildings near the US Embassy were other embassies and other insular buildings but eventually she found an more metropolitan neighbor hood. There was an internet cafe on the corner. She still had a little money left from her stash. She could try to video chat with her father, or at least email him. He was American. He would know what to do; how to deal with the US Embassy.

Brett's phone beeped. The chief was debriefing the swing shift, giving out assignments for the day. It was early afternoon. The day shift hadn't come back yet and the night shift was still fast asleep at home. His phone beeped again and everyone turned to stare at him. It wasn't the usual sound his phone made: it was sort of swooshy; he was just as confused as everyone else.

"Sorry Chief. I'm not sure what's up. Phone doesn't usually sound like this..." He pulled out his phone and unlocked the screen: it was the video chat app. He never used it, except to talk to Gabriela.

"Chief, it's my daughter. Something's wrong. We always schedule our video calls. I've been real worried about her. Can I take this? She don't have internet often an' I can't call her back."

"If it's an emergency. Come talk to me in my office after—I'll catch you up."

Brett nodded and left the briefing room, pressing the green "accept call" button as soon as he got to the hallway.

Gabriela thought he wasn't going to pick up the call. It had been ringing for a while. She had started typing up an email while she waited. But, when she thought the video chat portal would tell her the call failed, he finally answered.

"Hi Gabby, what's up?"

"Dad. I need your help." She choked a little, trying not to cry.

"Sure thing. What can I do?"

"He threw me out. Mama gave me a little money she had saved. I'm in Bogotá. I went to the US Embassy, but they wouldn't help me because I don't have my Colombian papers. I don't know what to do. I can't go back. What do I do?"

"Oh Gabby, are you ok? You look terrible. Did he hit you?" She nodded.

"That's why I can't go back."

"Ok. Here's what we'll do. I'll book a hotel for you in Bogotá. Can you stay at the internet cafe and check your email again in an hour or so? I need to talk to the Chief, but I'll fly out there to get you. I insisted your mom give me your original birth certificate, and when I visited when you were two I got a paternity test, so I have proof that you're my kid. So I'll bring all that and we'll go to the embassy together, Ok?"

She nodded.

"Right. Well, I'll talk to the chief and set up the hotel. I'll email you the details. Ok?"

She nodded again, and he ended the call. She paid and left, looking for something to do for an hour. There was a coffee shop on the corner of the next block. She was starving. She hadn't eaten since that one small serving of rice and beans the day before, and after Papa kicked her in the stomach she had vomited it out.

Brett knocked on the door to the Chief's office, entering after he heard a muffled "come in." The Chief looked up from his computer screen and saw Brett's face: jaw locked stubbornly, a concerned wrinkle in his forehead, and a defiant glint in his grey eyes.

"So. It was an emergency then."

"Definitely an emergency sir." Brett didn't ask how the Chief had figured that out. He'd been here long enough to know that the Chief always knew when something was up. "Her stepfather's beaten her up and she can't get papers from the embassy to move here. I'll need to request a few days leave, sir. I have to get her out of there. Honestly, I've been trying to get her to leave for years, but she wouldn't leave her mother."

"Ok. Do you have all the documents you'll need?"

"Yeah. I've got her birth certificate and the results of a paternity test. If that isn't good enough, I'm gonna get her a visitor's visa and then deal with the rest once she's here."

"I have a suggestion."

"Sir?"

"Take your old army uniform, the dress one with all your medals. Wear it to the embassy. Maybe it'll make an impression."

"Oh. I hadn't though of that. That's a good idea."

"Good luck, Brett. Let me know when you get back and I'll put you back into rotation."

"Thanks Chief. I appreciate it, really I do."

Brett closed the door behind him. He walked over and sat at his desk. He didn't have a computer of his own; if he needed one he used this one here. He sat and looked up flights and hotels. He picked a hotel and emailed the info to Gabby. The flight he found was a direct flight, but he wouldn't get there until the morning. It had been a long time since he'd taken a red-eye. Since he'd flown anywhere, really. He just got the one-way ticket. He would get a return ticket once he knew Gabby was coming back home with him.

Gabriela was surprised she didn't have trouble getting the room her father had reserved for her. She had spent the extra pesos to print out the reservation, and it seemed that had been a good idea. The room was huge. Their apartment in Cartagena could have fit inside it with room. There were two big beds and a private bathroom. And a private balcony.

The bathroom had fluffy white towels and two bathrobes. She took her clothes off and scrubbed and rinsed them in the sink. She hung her clothes to dry on the balcony railing before taking a shower herself The soap smelled like tourists, but she didn't mind. She would be clean. The hot water helped her relax a little, but seeing all her bruises brought back all her conflicting emotions.

She had deserted Mama, leaving her alone with nobody to protect her. She felt like a coward for running away to her father in the US. She was relieved that she didn't have to see Papa ever again. She was anxious: what if her father didn't have any luck at the embassy either? What if something happened to his flight? She was scared because she didn't really know what to expect once she got to Dallas.

Maybe she should have stayed in Cartagena; she knew what to expect there and she would have been able to visit Mama when Papa was at work. What if she was doing the wrong thing by leaving?

She turned on the TV, since it wasn't dark yet. She could practice her English so she wouldn't be totally lost in Dallas. She fell asleep in the middle of a soap opera, not noticing that the TV was still on. The re-runs continued to play until she woke up the next morning.

Someone was knocking on the door to the room. She got up and went to the door, making sure the robe was still securely tied around her waist. Then she undid the lock and bolt she had carefully set the evening before.

It was her father. He was tall. She had to crane her neck to see his face, which looked strange from below.

"Hi Gabby."

"Hi Dad."

She moved aside and let him in, closing and locking the door again. Brett sat down on the unused bed.

"Well, I thought we could get some breakfast and then get your papers at the embassy."

"Ok." She nodded. She picked up her clothes from the balcony—dry now—and went into the bathroom to put them back on. They were a little stiff, and there were a few rips she hadn't noticed before, but they were clean.

They ate downstairs in the hotel's restaurant and then took a taxi to the Embassy, which was much faster than walking had been. Gabriela ate as much as she could, which wasn't a lot. Her stomach was cramping with nerves. Maybe she would be able to eat again after everything was over. Brett saluted the guards, who saluted back. Once they were inside, someone led them to a different room, where another official sat at a desk.

"Sir. How can I help you and the young lady today?"

"My daughter needs a temporary passport so I can take her back to Dallas." Brett pulled out all the papers he had brought from the pocket inside the left of his jacket.

"This is her original birth certificate?"

"Yes."

"And a paternity test, and all your credentials. You're retired now? A cop?"

"Yeah. I was making a difference in the army. My mom was getting very ill so I needed to stay in Dallas with her and I wanted to continue helping my fellow citizens. It made sense to join the police force."

"And the bruising?"

"Her stepfather. That's what I'm trying to get her out for."

Gabriela tried to pay attention, but she didn't understand all their words and they mumbled.

"Does she have a social security number?"

"I don't know."

"Well, you'll have to get her one when you get back." The official turned to Gabriela. "I just need a picture of you to go with the temporary passport, ok?"

"Ok. What do I do?"

"Come stand in front of the wall over here. The background has to be white."

She looked at her father, he nodded encouragement, so she went and stood where the official pointed. He took the photo with his phone and tapped a few words into a message, before a tweet–like swoosh announced that it had been sent.

"Excellent. The documents should be printing now. One of the secretaries will bring it out to you."

"Thanks"

Brett gathered the papers and stood. They went back to the main entrance hall. They had only been waiting about ten minutes when a secretary brought them Gabriela's paperwork. Gabriela held her papers so tightly that had anyone wanted to take them away they would have had to rip them out of her hands. She had been so scared that she wouldn't get the documents she would need. Now a different set of worries ran through her mind: what if they changed their minds? The officers at the airport? What if they didn't let her into the US even though she had the papers?

The taxi was still waiting for them outside the embassy and they took it to the airport. Brett bought them tickets on the next flight out. It wasn't a full flight because most of the summer tourists left on the weekends and it was Tuesday. It was night when they got to Dallas. Most things were closed, but Brett stopped at a little diner so they could eat. Gabriela thought the city looked a lot like Cartagena at night, with all the bright lights decorating the skyscrapers. But here there weren't as many hills and no mountains to speak of. Brett's apartment was a small studio. He let Gabriela sleep on the bed. He usually slept on the reclining chair by the TV anyway.

Brett took Gabriela to the mall the next morning, since she hadn't brought anything but the clothes she was wearing. Gabi wasn't used to shopping for clothes herself. Mama had always found her clothing back in Cartagena, and clothes were passed down to her younger sisters as she outgrew them. Everything here was different. The food, the clothes, the polished squeaky floors. Air conditioning: it felt like winter inside. The air was dusty and dry without the saltiness of the Caribbean. She missed Mama and the smell of home. Brett was nice, and tried to help, but he didn't really understand.

Brett took her to a doctor in the afternoon. The doctor was shocked at the bruising, and said she was very lucky to have a father who would take her away. She agreed, but said she wished she could have saved Mama and her siblings too. The doctor said maybe she could, once she was all grown up. Gabriela didn't think so, but didn't say anything. Once the doctor had done all the tests and finished poking and prodding at her, she got a slip with some unintelligible writing and Brett took her to the pharmacist. They gave her some pills for parasites and some cream to put on the bruises to keep them from hurting. They stopped at the furniture warehouse on the way home and picked up a bed, a desk, and some drawers for Gabriela.

Brett talked to the apartment manager, and they moved down a floor to a two-bedroom apartment nearly three times the size of the studio apartment. Brett called in some of his cop buddies to help move the furniture and get everything set up. It didn't take long, and the new apartment remained sparse and bare. But it was good enough. Thursday Brett went back to work and Gabriela started at the local high school.

Brett was at the precinct Saturday night, on computer duty and manning the phone. He was taking the shift for the officer that had covered his shifts while he was bringing Gabby back and getting settled. It wasn't quite late enough for drunk calls or domestic disturbances, so he was sitting and fretting. He didn't have the faintest idea how to be a father, let alone to a teenage daughter whose customs were so different from what he was used to. She had asked about going to church tomorrow and he didn't even know where the closest Catholic church was.

He noticed Maria leaving.

"Maria, do you have a minute? I need your help. For Gabby."

"Sí. I heard you went to get her. She here?"

"Home," he nodded, "at the apartment. She has a lot of homework to catch up on. I think she's doing ok so far, though. But I don't know where to take her to church tomorrow and I don't know anything about the kinsaynera party you were telling me about. Her birthday is next week and I don't even know where to start. Can you help me?"

"She can come to church with me. I'll take her. Have her meet me at the bus stop on the corner at 9. I'll take her to get her dress and shoes too. You should get her a present: a necklace or nice earrings. I'll ask my cousin Jose if his restaurant is available Saturday night, then the music and food will be taken care of. Don't worry, it will be perfect. A little taste of home for your daughter, no?"

"Thank you Maria. I don't know what I would do without your help. I know this must be overwhelming for Gabby, but it's pretty overwhelming for me too. I never thought I would be raising her. I'm probably going to screw everything up, just like my dad."

"You be ok. Not like your dad at all. Don't

worry. Buena noche!"

"Bye. And thanks again."

By next Saturday, everything had been arranged. Brett drove Gabriela to Jose's restaurant. Maria had introduced Gabriela to everyone her age after church, so she was starting to make some friends. She was still painfully shy, but she didn't have to sit by herself at lunch anymore. Most of the people she met at church came to her party with their families, all dressed up and excited for her.

The restaurant smelled a little like home; the food used the same spices. It was nicer, cleaner, and reminded her more of the brightly colorful neighborhoods than the warren where Mama and Papa lived. The music was just the same: live instruments and music and dancers communicating in a complex, spontaneous, celebration.

When Brett brought her the high heels she had found with Maria, she realized he was just as uncomfortable in the spotlight as she was. That mad her feel better, and she started to relax. So she enjoyed the dancing, collecting her fifteen red roses from her father and the other young men she hardly knew. She only wished Mama were there to celebrate with her. Pictures would have to suffice. That night when she was home in her own bed—a big bed all to herself, in a room all to herself, the ultimate luxury—she promised herself that she would do whatever it took to make sure Mama and her siblings were safe.

Survivors of domestic violence face high rates of depression, sleep disturbances, anxiety, flashbacks, and other emotional distress.*

Fear is pain arising from the anticipation of evil.
— Aristotle

SEX ED 001

By Amelia Golden

Acute angle
Vice grip
Neck nape
Cheek floor
Eyes boggled
Twisted spine
Butt up
Cold exposed
Contracting as
Battering ramming
Ripping searing
Screaming anus
Penis piercing
Obliterating ownership
Broken body
Blood smearing

Dead tears
Raw knees
Freezing feet
Just a child
This is sex

SELF-RESPECT

By L. Meadow

When the iron fist
of your disregard
smashed my heart,
what poured forth
from the ruins
was not blood
or even tears,
but the purest light
of my regard for myself.

LULLABY

By Aurelia Maria Casey

Little brother, little brother
Sleep now, you are safe.
Daddy loves you,
Mommy loves you,
Sissy and me love you too.

Little brother, little brother
What did she do,
That woman that birthed you?
That you cling so tightly
To my hand to fall asleep
Yet you fight us all your waking hours.

Little brother, little brother
Sleep now, you are safe.
Daddy loves you,

Mommy loves you,
Sissy and me love you too.

Hush now little brother
It's my bedtime too.
Let go of my hand,
You're still safe without it.
I'll sing to you a little longer
So you'll know you're safe, you're safe.

Little brother, little brother
Sleep now, you are safe.
Daddy loves you,
Mommy loves you,
Sissy and me love you too.

Hush now little brother
We'll all protect you
Daddy and Mommy and Sissy and me.
Sleep and grow.
One day you'll be big enough
You can protect all the others too.

Little brother, little brother

Sleep now, you are safe.
Daddy loves you,
Mommy loves you,
Sissy and me love you too.

SOMATIC FLASHBACK

By Amelia Golden

I twist as I try to reach something while sitting on my comfy chair in the living room. The diagonal muscles at the bottom of my right frontal ribs spasm. I sit back quickly and puff my stomach out to try to relieve the cramp. It hurts. My back also aches, in the adrenal area. No stretching seems to make it better, but I try to massage the pains away. I am a little nauseous. When I attend to my stomach, I notice that it is bloated and painful. Not happy. I wonder what I have eaten that could have caused this, but my diet has been normal. There is a clenching in my intestines near the first abdominal spasm. I've had this in the past, and a chiropractor has told me that it is my ileo-cecal valve cramping shut. Great. Tugging on it doesn't help either. My intestines squirm, ache, push out at whatever is near. Things aren't moving through. There is no flow. There is a lot of gas: smelly, stinky gas. But even that won't come out. The pain from my abdomen makes my breathing shallow as it intensifies. I almost begin to hyperventilate. I can feel the spread of some kind of chemical over the top of my brain. It makes the top of my head feel a bit tingly. I am spacing out and getting anxious and wondering what am I to do? My abdominal muscles begin to convulse and heave, as if to vomit. I begin to shake and heave. My stomach muscles are going up and down in weird ways I have no control over. I hunch over, but then the vomiting reflex gets even stronger. I try to sit back, but I can't relax as my whole torso is in some strange spasm dance. I start to freak out. What should I do? What should I do? I try to breathe slowly, but I can't really, and my trying does not lessen the spasms. I can feel my heart beating fast now, and the bile rising up my throat. I'd gladly puke if there was only something to come out. I cough on mucous that is loosening from my sinuses and throat. I feel like I am choking on it. It disgusts me. My head pulls back and my head and neck shake and tremble quickly in a maddening shudder. I want away. I want out of this. Whatever it is, it is disgusting and I want out. I purposefully stop the gagging and try to breathe. One short breath. Another. Another. I can sit back a little now, though I am still shaky. I notice my tailbone against the chair. It hurts, it aches. I wonder why. As I attend to it, the pain becomes clearer like a solid memory. Pain, pain, pain. Aching that won't go away. A tailbone tensed out in hyper-defense. Now, it is not all the way out, but part-ways. Why? Why this, now, today? I can feel that my anus hurts and my whole rectum aches. Then, I remember. This morning, I had to poop but was (unusually for me) constipated. It wouldn't come out. It was hard and big, like a nasty man's penis. I just wanted it out, out, out. It took a very long time. Eventually, I could push it out, reminding me of birth pains. But it scraped me as it came out and made a bloody anal fissure. My butt is sore. It hurts and hurts. I pooped out that stupid penis of his. Pray to god it never comes back. Why must I live a life where every solid stool can't come out properly and triggers unconscious memories of anal rape? Why must I live a life where if I keep my stool soft, it leaks out into my underwear whenever I walk or move? Why can't the surgeons fix me? Why must I live with the consequence of others' deeds? Why must I experience the daily pain and agony from someone else's lustful thrusts? Thinking all this doesn't settle me down. In fact, the anxiety is still there and I go in and out of hyperventilation and various spasms. Now that I've figured out a couple probable triggers (pooping, post-nasal drip triggering the gag reflex, my daughter not being picked up by the school van at BART for community service, the fact that my mother called earlier in the day and re-confirmed her commitment to not remembering anything and that her life is just fine that way thank you) I know what is happening, and that calms me a little. My body is flooded with adrenaline. I get up and down. I can't think, I can't focus, I can't concentrate.

What should I do? I can't read. Everyone is gone, or almost so. If my son doesn't come home soon he will have to stay with me and miss the concert. It is already patently clear that I cannot go to our planned family outing. I get up again, pace, and call my husband. With a shaky voice, I remind him that I am not feeling well (in fact, I told him that earlier in the day). Then I say I am almost in a panic attack. Saying this out loud amplifies the panic and I go into full hyperventilation. I am worried about my son and the concert and my daughter who is out there on her own riding BART and not answering her cell phone. My son is not home! What should we do? The neighbors took him on an outing and promised to have him back by 5:30pm, but it is already past six. My husband says that I will have to watch our son this evening, because he needs to go soon. I panic more, as I feel so very unready to parent hyperactive Ricky when I myself am in a panic attack. At the last moment, my husband comes back in the house and tells me that Ricky has arrived and they are going to the concert. I can be alone. I can sit here and panic alone. This relieves me, some weight off my shoulders. I let myself tremble and shake. I let the tears and tears and tears drip down my face, salty sweet. I plead, "Why the pain, why the pain, why the pain?" I rock back and forth like a little child in disbelief. Why is this happening to me? Why me? What did I do to deserve this? Where is everybody? Why won't mother make things better? My consciousness flits back and forth between here and then, here and then, whenever and now and what am I to do? It is time to eat dinner but I can't stomach the thought of putting anything into my body. I pace. My eyes must look wild. I don't know what to do. I can't think. There is nothing to do. Time is empty. It is getting dark. The cats do not react to all the noise I am making. I can't cuddle them or find them. I wonder if I should try to snap myself out of it by dumbing out on TV. But there are only crime shows to watch, not exactly the most calming thing. I sit in the den, get up, sit in there again, try to get the cats to come to me, give up, shut the door, sit, breathe, breathe. And I turn on the TV. And it is gruesome and tense and familiar. I let my breathing slow and my crying drip down. I huddle the great big panda I got myself last Christmas, hugging it tight as can be, leaning against his head. I numbly watch the story lines go by. After a few shows, I am calmer and figure I must eat or I will get worse. The thought of food still upsets me. But I figure I have to eat something, or my blood sugar will drop even more and I will just fall apart. So I manage to get some puffed millet and cover it with soy milk. It is tasteless. I eat it down and feel some sense of accomplishment. When the show is over, I go upstairs and take a hot bath. I am so exhausted. I hear people arriving home during my bath. I am too tired to greet them. I am too tired by the time I am out of the bathtub to even check on the little one. I simply creep under the covers and huddle until my consciousness is blissfully wiped clean.

I AM MORE

By L. Meadow

I am more…

> …than a collection of differentiated cells
> …than the sum total of bone, tissue, muscles and internal organs
> …than the organic and inorganic working of my brain
> …than a collection of my memories
> …the sum total of my experiences
> …than the list of my qualifications
> …than a wife, a mother, a sister, a child
> …than people expect

because I am me!

ON THE CAPE OF NO HOPE

By Daniela Thions-Meyer

I planted my flag on the cape of no hope and stood on the rocks by the ocean. I took a deep breath and in a defying bellow I told of the things that brought me there. I told about the soldiers who, for us, went out to die; about the heroes of disasters and the refugees of life. I demanded explanations for the things I have inside: the hidden rage, the fallen hopes, the dried out tears, this mending heart. I asked about the solitude and why it was my friend? I prayed for the forgotten, the forsaken and the lost. For the tireless workers who lost sight of the changing times, for the lonesome leaders who enjoy the views from up above but are all too often alone. I asked about compassion, where it went and when it would come back...

With every question I asked, the ocean of resignation grew darker and calmer. My words of hate, my tortured cries, carried by a wind too cold, too empty, resonated in the calmness of this desolate place. Feeding off its own echo, my anger grew louder and louder, all I could feel was my pounding heart and the bitter taste of losing everything I ever held so dear.

So I took every ounce of fear, and pain, and anger, every wound ever inflicted upon me by an evil soul, every regret, every frustrated desire to act. I dug deep into my soul and collected the last of the strength within me and I begged the sea for answers. Answers for the untried murders, the ignored cries for help; I wanted to have a word of comfort for every innocent inmate, every scapegoat, every beaten single mother and every strong soul who has lost the power to read, laugh, see, sing, listen… A moment of silence for every child soldier, every selfless warrior who lost the will to try. Finally in the silence I asked about the artists, whose names were lost in history's disdain, the poets whose words died before their time.

That night, I learned the formula for producing more tears where I thought there were none left, because it was really worth crying. Then, as if answering my pleas, a wave formed and crashed upon me, drenching me in the waters of resignation; protesting against the apathy and numbness I had developed from this pain.

That night I learned that cowardice is for men, not for dreamers. Cowardly dreams don't make it to history, they just fade. There is no hope for them, memory can't save them, nor can the best troubadour deliver them right. I will not be this! Would I tolerate being a soon forgotten hero? Or would I be the fool of all the emptiness? So I decided to conquer the world in my own way. I have everything I need to do it: a train that is late, a movie ticket from a different era, a book with no story and a skeletal memory. There is a plate in my house with a solitary strawberry and a pot of jam the flies won't approach. I know a place where a flower has died in the water that once made it live and a map to a place that no longer exists. I am armed with Voltaire and the Little Prince, my crooked spoon and my blue rain boots. I have the drawing you made of the dreams that I had and the words that describe the moments we have not yet lived. I hold in my hand your forgotten acts of kindness, our gentle words of love. I have the model, the blueprints of every torn down city, every collapsed empire and the logic behind every faltering ideology. I have every reason to be upset, every right to be enraged and an aching desire to be free. I had a child's disguise to hide my mission and a passion ready to materialize, with time; I have found a dream that changes color and a life that spins to evolution.

Know, and don't doubt, that I will stand where all else has fallen, I will bow to every monument of strength. And, in the thick fog of this destruction, you will see me standing strong, for I will not be defeated. I will collect the tears of strangers to understand the roots of sorrow; I will rise from the ashes of this crumbling universe. I will not allow my soul to raise monsters before me but will be prepared to vanquish them, and that I will! The demons that haunt me today will be defeated tomorrow. But most importantly, I will love; I will laugh; I will remember. I will call this world my home and I will extend my hand to anyone willing to shake it. I have a trunk full of memories and I am moving on; for across this ocean lies a place some will surely call heaven. And if it takes years to sail the waters that will lead me there, I will learn the maps to reach it. The adventure will be long and I will not look back on the ones who led me here. I will learn to forgive and I will learn to find the words that, without telling anyone where I heard them, will heal the wounds you thought would never heal. I will find the chords that will come to reignite the fires that once burned deep in the hearts of all who have been defeated. And I will bring passion and reason to those who, in a moment of weakness, lower their gaze and drag their lonely, battered pride to plant their flag on the cape of no hope.

Without help, girls who witness domestic violence are more vulnerable to abuse as teens and adults.*

Without help, boys who witness domestic violence are far more likely to become abusers of their partners and/or children as adults, thus continuing the cycle of violence in the next generation.*

"Hope is the thing with feathers
That perches in the soul
And sings the tune without the words
And never stops at all."
— Emily Dickinson

RESOURCES

In this section I have included a few resources for victims and survivors of domestic violence. I have tried to balance lists of agencies with information to develop necessary skills for independence. The only policy I know enough about to mention is specific to the US, but I hope that those policies can stand as inspiration for countries that don't have similar policies. For each resource I wrote a few words about my experience with the website, highlighting what I think works and what it is best for. Please note that these are my opinions, and your experience may differ.

If I did not include a resource that you think is important or if you want to let me know about your experience with one of these

resources, please email me at aurelia@amcasey.
com. I will use any feedback I receive to modify
and update the resources section for the 2015
anthology.

HOT PEACH PAGES

www.hotpeachpages.net

This website has lists of abuse agencies by region and country worldwide. There's a lot of information, so it can take some searching to find the right organization for your needs. They also have information about domestic violence in many languages which can be essential when you are trying to help someone who is only comfortable with their own language. They have a chart that shows which languages they have available, so if you don't find your language consider helping them out by writing or translating something yourself.

If you are worried about someone finding Hot Peach Pages (or any of the other websites listed here) in your browser history, they have information on internet safety on their

SurfSavvy! page: http://www.hotpeachpages.
net/a/surfsavvy.html

NATIONAL COALITION AGAINST DOMESTIC VIOLENCE

www.ncadv.org

This website has info about supporting domestic violence awareness, questions to ask yourself if you aren't sure that you're being abused, and a page with some basic questions to ask when you are talking to a lawyer. They have resources for financial education, cosmetic and reconstructive surgery, and identity protection. It's really comprehensive, I just wish it were a little more intuitive to navigate.

WOMEN'S LINK WORLDWIDE

www.womenslinkworldwide.org

This website is a great Spanish language resource. There seems to be a large number of articles with the same breadth of information as the NCADV but focused more globally. If you are in Latin America, Spain, or other Spanish speaking communities this will be a valuable source of information. They have hotline numbers for their offices in Madrid and Bogota listed at the bottom of their website.

WOMEN'S AID

www.womensaid.org.uk

This is the UK equivalent to the NCADV. They have information on how to get help in the UK as well as news about their most recent awareness campaigns. If you're living in the UK this is the first place to go to learn about domestic violence laws and policies in the UK and how you can get the help you need.

U.S. POLICIES ABOUT DOMESTIC VIOLENCE

There are a number of important domestic violence laws in the US. VAWA, the violence against women act, was reauthorized in 2013. This is the document that governs where the lines are between bad behavior and criminal behavior with regard to physical and sexual abuse. You can find a lot of information on VAWA 2013 with a simple google search, including the actual bill itself. It provides comprehensive protection, so in addition to women and children the bill covers male victims, the LGBT community, and Native Americans living on reservations.

Most major cities in the US have women's shelters and men's shelters. Often people assume these shelters are resources for the homeless, and they do a lot of work with the homeless. However, the women's shelters have a strong focus on helping women escape domestic violence. Many women's shelters will take children with their mothers, although the age limit for boys can be a problem. Most of these shelters keep their location secret, so you have to look them up and call them to make use of their services or to volunteer to help them.

One of the most common actions taken against an abuser is to issue a restraining order. The distance indicated can vary, and enforcement can be an issue, but it provides grounds for legal action if the abuser disregards the restraining order. Laws and requirements vary by state. However, one important but often overlooked federal law is that anyone who has been accused of domestic violence (the abuser) automatically has his or her right to firearms revoked. It is important that you make sure your abuser gets listed in the directory so gun and ammunition sellers know not to sell to your abuser. Also, there is no guarantee that any firearms that your abuser already possesses will be removed. Remember, enforcement and interpretation of these laws varies from state to state.

Find legal advice in your state. There should be free options, but be aware that they may take a long time to get around to your case.

Domestic violence victims lose nearly 8 million days of paid work per year in the US alone—the equivalent of 32,000 full-time jobs.**

"There is a saying in Tibetan, 'Tragedy should be utilized as a source of strength.'
No matter what sort of difficulties, how painful experience is, if we lose our hope, that's our real disaster."
— Dalai Lama XIV

ACKNOWLEDGMENTS

Without the help of the following people, this anthology would never have seen the light of day.

My parents, for letting me bounce ideas off them. Especially my mom for helping to spread the word about submissions.

And most importantly, all the contributing authors. Your willingness to respond to a call for submissions at the last minute enabled me to follow through to make this anthology exist this year.

ABOUT THE AUTHORS

MIMI BLAKE

Mimi Blake has lived all over the US, but she calls the Pacific Northwest Home. She has a great many tattoos. She can't decide which she favors most; the sugar-skull with bullets for teeth or the tree with a quote beneath it by Pablo Neruda. She's been writing twenty-seven years, although Mimi doesn't consider herself a writer. She's attended workshops facilitated by Julie Glover, Danez Smith, Jeffrey McDaniel, and many others. This is her first-ever submission. She overcomes adversity by reminding herself that someone else always has it worse. She's discovered this through poetry. "It's validating" Mimi says "you can see, you literally can see. I don't know how to explain it—you can see a bird in their pen-stroke—I don't know how else to explain it. It's like Pablo Neruda describing bread; you just know that bread is the love of his life." Mimi Blake sees herself as not just a Survivor, but a warrior; fighting until she wins. Mimi now resides in Richmond, Virginia with her husband and two daughters.

A.C.

A.C. was born in Europe and moved to London, UK, in the mid-sixties. Her mother was effectively a single parent at a time when this was very much frowned upon. Her father did not provide financial support. Her parents eventually divorced in the Seventies. AC is an English graduate with an MSc in an IT subject. She sees herself as either a dilettante or an aspiring Everywoman, depending on how she's feeling at the time.

AURELIA MARIA CASEY

I write fiction, short stories, and poetry. Most of my fiction and short stories are fantasy, while most of my poetry is inspired more directly by actual events in my life. I love imagining new worlds and learning about characters by learning their stories. I often find myself asking questions as I write that lead to enough material for prequels just because I wanted to know something of the history behind that story.

In addition to writing, I do almost anything creative including but not limited to drawing, sewing, cooking, and dancing. I love to read, any good story in any genre, and I love to travel. Maybe someday I'll even find a place to call home.

You can read my blog and find my other work at www.amcasey.com

AMELIA GOLDEN

Amelia Golden is a writer, educator, psychologist and musician. She shares a house in California with her husband, two Abyssinian cats, complicated computer wiring, and too many books, with occasional visits from her three children. Her inner children assert that it is their home too, though they don't have dedicated bedrooms. Her family is committed to stopping the cycle of abuse. Now. They'd appreciate some help in this endeavor, as well as greater awareness of the public about the profound soul murder that results from child sexual abuse.

L. MEADOW

L. Meadow is an avid movie watcher, insane reader, photographer, and writer. Mostly she enjoys writing lighthearted, funny or uplifting short stories with a small twist in the tale and poetry. Once in a while she opens the dark box in the back of her head and lets out the memories stored there, but only when necessary, as her journey to healing has taken her far past those memories into a place of self-acceptance. There comes a time in your journey when you need to stop looking backwards at the old life that has gone and start looking forwards to the new life that has come.

She has published two short story collections *Take 2* and *Seeds in a Pod,* and one anthology of poetry, *Small Eyes, Wise Eyes,* and is hard at work putting the finishing touches on a fantasy novel *Dragon Soars, Phoenix Dances.*

She shares her life with a few beloved friends and family, a white rat and one large black cat who rules the roost, as all cats tend to do, having never forgotten they were once worshiped as gods.

You can find more of her writing at https://sites.google.com/site/meadow337writes/

DANIELA THIONS-MEYER

Daniela Thions-Meyer is a consultant in Mexico City, where she hopes to have a positive impact on her city. She has been writing for years and is particularly interested in writing fiction and short stories. Her passions include understanding people, hosting, reading and working on her little house in the mountains.

PAUL WHITE

I am a novelist, short story writer (including flash fiction), poet, article writer, and blogger.

My writing covers various genres and topics including life, love, emotions, depression, trauma, suspense, sex, romance, social and world issues.

All my writing features the most important matter of all, the human condition. The hopes, dreams and fears, the self-doubt, and uncertainties that lie within all of us. These issues are portrayed through the characters that inhabit the worlds within the pages of my Novels and Short stories. They are reflected in my poetry and various essays in my blogs and social media posts.

As for myself....well I have a warped and varied sense of humour, I love good food, good wine and good company.

I'm an ardent independent traveller, nature lover, and supporter of ecological and wildlife preservation.

My home is in God's own country, the county of Yorkshire, England, where I live with my wife and ancient cat.

I have a website where you can read more about what projects I am currently working on, http://fluffybunnypj.wix.com/paul-white and read some of my past works on the SHOW-CASE page. Please feel free to visit at any time.

According to the U.S. Department of Housing and Urban Development, domestic violence is the third leading cause of homelessness among families.*

"Hope is not about proving anything. It's about choosing to believe this one thing, that love is bigger than any grim, bleak shit anyone can throw at us."
— Anne Lamott

ENDNOTES

Quotes were taken from:
www.goodreads.com

* statistics are from from:
http://www.safehorizon.org/page/
domestic-violence-statistics--facts-52.html

**statistics are from from:
http://domesticviolencestatistics.
org/domestic-violence-statistics/

www.ingramcontent.com/pod-product-compliance
Lightning Source LLC
Chambersburg PA
CBHW070502170726
48291CB00008B/2624